BRUJERÍA

Valentina Arango

BRUJERÍA

Valentina Arango

Ediciones *El Pozo*
Oneonta, New York

Cover art:
Andrés Felipe Moreno Toro

Ediciones El Pozo
37 Fairview Street, apt 4
Oneonta, New York
13820. USA

ISBN: 978-0-9861812-7-6

Printed in U.S.A.

For Mateo

The day my grandfather died was uneventful. He lay on his bed sleeping to the hum of a soccer match on the radio. For several hours, after the match had ended, the radio played through paid programming and news. I thought the stillness of the house normal. But when night came, and he had not moved, I walked over to his bed. I had never seen a dead man before.

One

I walk over to the counter, and point to the shelf behind the round lady, "I'll have a cigar." She reaches over, turns back around, punches some numbers into the cash register, and says in a high-pitched voice, "You know, these are bad for you, young man." She fumbles with the cigar, slides it across to me, and takes my coin.

I have a long walk ahead, and the night only makes the trip more dangerous. Wearing a light grey manta is no help; someone could easily spot me and try to mug me. I would be killed since all I have is some change. I walk down the road further and further away from the tienda. Darkness soon envelops me. I light the cigar and begin the prayer, the one my grandfather taught me, "It calls our ancestors, las ánimas, to walk with you. There's so many of them, no one dares to come near you."

The smoke rises around me, and any one seeing me walking tonight would swear there was a group of at least fifty people. The cigar is also a way to measure how far one travels. Before meters and kilometers, people measured their distances by the number of tobaccos they would smoke.

I arrive at the town, just as daylight is breaking in. No more than thirty houses, made of adobe walls and tin roofs, are scattered along the trodden dirt road. I put out what is left of my cigar. I tuck the stub into my shirt pocket, and make my way to the only spot that is open this early in the morning. It is a small shack with a withered roof of palm leaves, and frame of guadua wood. Under the fragile shelter was a thick lady, beads of sweat glisten on her dark skin as she stands over a pan of hot cooking oil.

Beside the little kitchen under the misty morning air there are two tables, and four chairs. I sit in the sturdiest looking one, which nonetheless wobbles under my weight. She brings over a small plastic cup, and she serves me tinto. I sit and look across the way, at the palm trees and picture the ocean that is on the other side. I wish I could abandon my trip, if only for a moment, jump through the trees, and reach the ocean.

I remember those days by the beach when I was content with the sight of the ocean, the smell of the fish, and the sound of the stories my grandfather told as he clipped his fingernails. He told me many tales of his wild and rebellious youth. One of those times he slammed down the clippers, and in a lower voice he spoke, "When I was eleven, we were living in a small town near San José del Nuz. They were very religious there. I never was. But, one time, I stole this book that was banned by the Church. If anyone found out that I read it they would kick me out of the town, and excommunicate me. It was bad. I sat there reading this book by Vargas Vila, it was night, so I was huddled around the candle, when all of a sudden I felt something pushing up from under my bed. It scared me half to death, but I had to look, to see if anyone was playing a trick on me. I looked and there he was, the Devil himself. Two golden eyes staring back at me. I wanted to scream, but I knew that would only bring me more misfortune. I blew out the candle, and went under the covers." He grabbed the nail clipper again, and began to chuckle.

I come back from my dreams, finish the tinto, give the lady the last of my money, and continue up the dirt road. The directions are simple, too simple. I know visiting this Indian mamo is a part of the ceremony, I just can't understand why it is only me on this trip, and why the entire family depends on it. My mother tried to explain, as she rubbed the different herbal waters over me, "Can't you feel it, hijo? The negativity is all around us. First, your father leaves us, now your aunt is going blind, and the birds! The birds. They're on a suicide rampage!" She crossed herself, reached over for the last of the herbal water, continued praying to the saints, and in small splashes doused me with the water. I know it is something I have to do, but I sense that this is going to be far bigger than anyone has prepared me for.

I reach the steps of the modern brick home of El Mamo and ring the doorbell. Soft, barefoot steps approach the door, a little girl, no more than seven years old, with bright green eyes looks me up and down. I feel bulky and intrusive. I take off my zapatos, and she extends her hand to receive my manta. I walk down the green corridor, with the pictures of different family members. I try to guess which one is El Mamo, but by the time I reach the second door, the little girl yanks my hand. I stop and look down, at her. She motions me toward her, and so I bow to listen.

The girl whispers "Don't let the evil fool you, keep on your path, Teomio. The whispers of the birds come from her lips, and through her eyes. In a moment, I am stunned. I am lost in her eyes, and in her whispers that yank my memories from within me, and suddenly, her eyes turn a gentle grey, like the smell of smoke in the air. From the other room I hear a woman shout, "Valen, por andar enchimbada dejó quemar los fríjoles." The little girl bounces away giggling, and disappears into another room.

Back at home, my backyard is a small version of a forest. The rubber trees are home to the most colorful birds, the iguanas and even the porcupines. Locals use the trees for fishing. This forest was unaltered and protected nature. However, it came at a price; we constantly received threats from those trying to turn our little plot of wilderness into Valledupar's new attraction for tourists. We protected it against everyone. As a child, I would run into the forest, with my cousins to hunt for iguanas. I was the best at capturing them. I would sit for hours catching them and releasing them again. I respected them. They were here long before us. My cousins and uncles all thought I was crazy for letting them go again especially on the nights there was only rice to eat.

"Come in!" the voice screams from the other side of the door. El Mamo is wearing jeans, a Metallica T-shirt, and Converse shoes. He stands in the corner, at the other end of the room, with a stack of books in his hands, "Close the damn door and hurry I don't have all day." I shut the door and walk toward the desk, careful not to knock over any of the many piles of books scattered all over the dim room. El Mamo looks at me and lets out a loud, "Tsk, tsk, tsk. If it isn't bad enough that you are thirty, you are also unmarried, and have no kids. Dammit they always do this to me. Here." El Mamo hands me a folded paper. As I look down and begin to open it, El Mamo shouts, "No, you idiot, you have to wait till you are at the river by the blue rock, and in the full moon! Just follow the creek. Now go. Get out."

I try to speak, but can't. I walk back through the door, and as I am closing it behind me, I look back, El Mamo is throwing books down, and they fall into neat piles.

I put on my zapatos and manta outside. I feel the warmth of the sun, but begin to shiver. It is about noon, I have no more money, and nowhere to go but the creek. The full moon is not for another two weeks. I head up the road, forcing myself not look back at El Mamo's house. The further I walk the less anxious I feel. I walk and listen to the leaves and sticks crackling under my boots. I begin to hear the creek coming closer. What did he mean by all that? I had forgotten that I was still grasping the thin paper, and when I remember I reach for my wallet, and put the paper in its little pocket. I place my wallet in my back pocket, and when I reach into my shirt for the stub of tobacco, I feel something different. A two thousand-pesos coin and I feel a little better. I know the ceremony has begun, and this coin is only the beginning of my family's change of luck. Now I can buy some food, and another cigar.

I walk on and I feel the moist air. I climb over the rocks, and land on the soft and muddy riverbank. I set down my manta, fold it into a pillow, and fall into a deep sleep.

I sit up from the long nap. The bank by the creek feels cool and refreshing. The soft sounds of the trees and the water flowing over the rocks, the birds singing into the quiet afternoon. I pick up the manta, shake the bits of ground away, fold it in half and throw it onto my shoulder. My stomach starts to grumble, I haven't eaten anything since my journey began, two whole days and all I had was some tinto. I stand up, pat the dirt from my clothes, walk over to the creek and drink, and then wash my face and neck with scoops of ice-cold water that runs down from the Sierra. I climb over the rocks by the bank, and make my way into town.

I step inside the small nameless restaurant and sit at one of the three tables. The darkness of the place leaves me blind for a few seconds while my eyes try to adjust. A thin boy, of about ten comes from the back room, serves me some water in a tin cup, and asks, "What will you have?"

I take the coin from my shirt pocket, and hand it to him, "One empanada, please." He eyes the coin suspiciously, takes out a pocketknife and tries to pierce a hole through the coin. When the blade does not go through, he nods, pockets the coin, and disappears into the kitchen.

Moments later, he reappears with my empanada, hot sauce and my change. My mouth begins to overflow; I feel like a savage for wanting to wolf down the empanada in one bite. I look over, and the boy is staring at me expressionless. I tear off a piece and slowly chew the meat potato filling. I don't know when I'll eat next, so I have to savor it.

When I am about half done with my banquet, a clamorous noise outside grows louder and louder. I look into the bright doorway at the empty street. After a few moments, a small blue minivan pulls up and from it two tall thick men with dark sunglasses emerge. The little boy, who had not lifted his eyes from me, suddenly stands up and walks to the driver. The man hands him a coin and he takes out his knife and checks the coin. They walk inside and the boy points them to a table.

The last time I rode in a minivan like that was when the guys and I decided to road trip to Cabo de la Vela. It was about five years ago. Right after all the Christmas celebrations. We were completely broke, but for some reason we decided that it was a good idea. Jacob borrowed the little minivan from a pal that owed him a favor. The damn thing was covered with hippie decals, and falling apart. That's where my bad luck began.

Two

"Get everything packed, don't forget my toilet paper and tooth brush," shouted Jacob at his wife, Lucia, who was in the other room with their two-year-old son, Damian, busily packing for the three of them. Jacob was almost seven feet tall and towered over the rest of us. His legs were like the trunks of trees, his neck alone was said to have the strength of ten men. Lucia was the opposite; she was short and very thin, and her hair flowed past her waist. We walked outside toward the minivan. It was already dark and close to midnight.

"Shouldn't we wait till the morning? I don't think it's a good idea to leave Santa Marta at night," I suggested to Jacob.

"Believe me, we do not want to be caught in morning traffic, and don't worry we are making a pit stop at the finca, from there we will leave in daylight."

I handed my bag to Caleb, who was standing on top of the car tying all the bags down. Caleb was the family lawyer. He was the only brown Jewish person I knew, and was always strutting around preaching; that and Manischewitz wine were all he talked about.

I stepped into the car, took out my wallet and Caleb, Jacob and me gathered 400 thousand pesos. For a road trip that would just about cover gas and meals and not much else. How we were going to make it, none of us knew. I cut the money in half put one-half in my wallet, then a fourth in my shoe and the last cut in my pocket. At that moment Red, Jacob's friend, came from the house carrying his small bag, and the big one Lucia had packed. Everyone called him Red because he lost a bet once and had to dye his hair red. It only stayed red about a week, but the name stuck. He told us his real name once, but no one cared to remember it. He passed the bags to Caleb, and the two of them finished tying them down.

Jacob walked back inside the house, while the rest of us waited by the car. I led Lucia and Damian into the back seat. Caleb stepped over, and put the bag with the Manischewitz, and plantain chips under the seat and then sat next to Lucia and Damian.

Red walked over next to me and said, "You sit by the door, and I'll sit in the middle, because I know Sirius wants the window seat." Sirius was a majestic pit-bull, that all the neighbors feared, who would cry at the sight of the stray cats and would hide under the bed during thunderstorms and family arguments.

"What about the front seat?" I asked.

"Didn't Jacob tell you? We're picking Luis up." Jacob came out of the house with Sirius on a leash, locked the door, and we all filed into the car. Luis was Jacob's friend. He was a Anglican priest, and a freemason. Similar to Caleb, Luis was always going on about his religion and spilling the secrets of the Freemasons. The lawyer and the priest did not get along; every time you put them into the same room, they were at each other's throats.

Jacob pulled up to Luis's house just two blocks away. The chubby priest came out with a small backpack, and sat in the front seat. In a posh accent he announced, "Hello ladies and gents. Let us begin our journey," and so we began.

About two hours into our trip, Jacob shook me awake, and said, "Hey man you take the wheel and take us the rest of the way, I'm fighting with my eyelids over here." He pulled over, everyone continued to sleep as he and I switched places. I guided the car, packed with the sleeping road-trippers, to the finca.

When we arrived, it was still dark. We got out of the car and stretched. Even the dog was happy to be out and roaming around the countryside. A sleepy couple, Lucia's parents, greeted us. The smiling pair hugged Lucia, and then shook hands with the rest of us. We found chairs scattered around the yard, and gathered in a circle. Lucia whispered to her mom, "Sorry to wake you, we wanted to stop by on our way to Cabo."

"Cabo? What on earth are you going to do there?" Lucia was nineteen, and her mother spoke to her as you would a misbehaving ten year old.

Lucia's father walked by the side of the house. He was about sixty. I stood up from the still sleepy group and followed him. He was collecting several buckets, and I asked, "Can I help you with anything?"

"Son, have you ever milked a cow before?" No I had not, but what the hell did he have to sound so patronizing for, who was he to judge.

"No, but I'm a fast learner." He scoffed and handed me two buckets. When we made it to the gate, we heard Jacob yelling after us.

"Wait for me!" He was running up with a flashlight, lighting the way so as to not step in any cow crap. He was so big and looked so damn awkward, running toward us. Jacob was followed by the laughing red head with a camera, and Lucia with a stool. The old man swung the gate open and locked it again behind us. He then patted several of the calves until he found one he liked and led it to the second gate. The little calf ran through the crowd of cows and found its mother. We followed the man into the corral and he tied the cow's two hind legs together. He grabbed the stool from Lucia and placed it by the cow, then placed a bucket under the cow and motioned me into the stool. I sat down and looked over at Jacob and Red. Red had the camera out ready to take pictures, and Jacob was preoccupied with keeping his sneakers clean.

I milked that damn cow like I had never milked anything before. Well, actually the poor cow probably thought I was ripping its teats off, but I got a good rhythm going after a few seconds, I filled that bucket about a tenth of the way. Meanwhile, Red was snapping pictures. The more we laughed the angrier the old man got. After a bit of yanking and an obnoxious photo-shoot I got tired, and Lucia declared it her turn.

She sat in the stool and said proudly, "Guys, this is how you milk a cow!" She filled the bucket almost half way. She was milking fast as hell. At that moment, a commotion came from the other side of the corral.

"Oh, no sudden movements, that's the bull there." Great, this old man was insane. Who puts a group of jumpy amateurs into a pen with a bull? At the sound of the bull, the cow tried to shift positions, and down went Lucia, and all the milk. Her bony legs flew into the air. It was the funniest shit in the world, but we couldn't laugh.

Lucia's dad was pissed, he led us to the gate and we gladly made our way back to the house, as the sun came up. Once we reached the house, Lucia's mother had made us arepas with cheese for breakfast. The Jewish lawyer and the Anglican priest were already starting to argue.

"Come on guys, don't start now," said Red, as he bit into the cheesy core of the arepa.

"This doesn't concern you. We all know your soul is dammed and you don't care," The Priest turned blue with anger. Red shrugged his shoulders and walked away from them.

"See, that's your problem. You're always damming people to hell, there's no progress in that," Caleb shouted as he stood up to serve himself some milk. Red walked into the van's back seat, laid out his towel, and took a nap.

In just a couple of hours, we were semi-rested, semi-fed and ready to continue our trip. We all got in the car, and drove off.

It was noon, and the sun was bright. The temperature was just starting to rise and I felt sweaty and gross. We decided to make a quick stop in

Valledupar, while Jacob and Luis took the car in for an oil change, they dropped us off by the Guatapuri river, the one with the Golden Mermaid statue on it. At the river, all you had to do was buy some snacks and drinks and you could sit in one of the tables. We bought a few packs of lemon-flavored chips, a six-pack of beer and some sodas. We took turns guarding the stuff, and taking dips in the river.

After about an hour of freshening up, Jacob and Luis picked us up and we were on our way yet again.

Once we were out of Valledupar, and on the highway, everyone seemed to relax. The trip was finally beginning, and our bodies and energies seemed cleansed. The Sierra Nevada appeared to our right as we passed several small pueblos.

At just about six, we hit a pothole and the car broke down. We were at least twenty minutes outside of town by car, and right smack in between two plantain fields. Now, unless you've actually been by these fields, you don't know how brutal the jején are. The jején are cousins of the mosquitos, but the little things are deadly. They smell new skin and attack it like a vicious pack of dogs. They don't sting you they take bites. Only ten minutes by the road, and every piece of exposed skin looked like a bad case of chicken pox. We decided to split up and hitchhike into town; it was our only hope since we were such a large group. I took a small car with Lucia and Damian first. Jacob and Luis followed in a car that stopped for them. The lawyer and the redhead waited with the dog by the car. We reached the small town, found a small cheap bug ridden motel, and rented out the only two rooms with air-conditioning.

Lucia, Damian and I made our way into the tiny room, with one full size bed and a small twin size cot. I turned the air and television on and lay in the cot. Lucia sat Damian next to me and frantically fixed herself. The news reported some roads that were blocked off by guerilla, and towns were violence of paracos was rampant. It was all very depressing so I turned it off.

The two women were fixing their hair and doing their makeup, I handed them the kid and decided to explore the town a bit. I stepped outside, and saw Luis and Jacob making their way toward me. They needed 50 thousand for a tow truck and mechanic. "We can be back on the road by tomorrow noon." Luis and I met with Caleb and Red to bring the bags back to the hotel, and have the car towed to the shop. And so, we all went out for dinner.

The next morning, I woke up with a hangover. I sat up, counted our money and we were down to our last 200 thousand pesos, I handed these to Jacob and he secured them in his belt pack. My head was *throbbing. After dinner, we had stopped by the hotel. Jacob, Caleb and I had a couple of drinks, and then got carried away with the rum. I took a cold shower in a damp and moldy bathroom, changed my clothes and went to pick up the minivan with Red. By the time we returned, everyone had showered and packed. The Lawyer climbed on the car again and tied down our bags; we had a small breakfast of empanadas and began our journey again on 180 thousand pesos.*

Three

I finish my empanada thank the young girl and make my way out of the adobe restaurant. I walk past the blue minivan, to a small convenience store and buy a cigar with the last of my change. I start to make my way back to the creek, and take out the small piece of paper El Mamo had given me. I try to see what is written inside it, but I know I am not supposed to open it until the full moon, so I place it back in my wallet. I reach the riverbank, sit down, light the cigar and notice that my box of matches is full. (I thought there were only a few matches left). The smoke and prayer not only protects me from muggers, but it also keeps bad spirits and bugs away.

Four

At around seven, we reached Maicao, a small town on the border of Venezuela and Colombia, where booze and gasoline are cheaper. It was almost dark and many of the stores were already closed. We managed to find one where we bought three cans of ham, one box of crackers, four packs of cigarettes and 6 bottles of tequila. Yes, that's right, instead of real food we bought canned ham, and instead of stocking up on food we stocked up on booze and smokes.

After we bought our nourishments, we filled up the car with some real cheap gasoline by the side of the road. Only about two more hours of road and we would arrive. While Red and Caleb gassed up the car, Jacob and I walked over to a small store because the canned ham gave us the shits. But, Lucia forgot the toilet paper back at the hotel.

"You were in charge of two damn things, my toilet paper and the kid! It's a goddamn miracle you didn't

leave him behind. What the hell are we going to do now?" he shouted and waved his hands at her. The tequila sure as hell didn't quiet him down. He was on a bloody drunken rant over the damn toilet paper. Lucia just cried and yelled back at him. Until finally she just started walking away from him.

I have known Jacob for many years, but I have never seen him get as pissed as he got when she walked away from him. Their arguing resolved nothing, I still needed to crap. "I'll be right back!" I shouted as I grabbed the keys from him and ran to the closest convenience store. I bought one roll of toilet paper and then ran into the store's bathroom to take care of business. When I walked back to the car Jacob was down the road following Lucia and screaming like a mad man.

He looked back and saw I had returned, he jogged back, out of breath he took the keys from me. The rest of us jumped in as he sped the car toward Lucia. We kept trying to say shit like, "Hey man, relax, slow down." He pulled up next to her, jumped out of the car, and forced her in. He sped off barely staying on the road, and pulled up to the bus station.

"One ticket to Minca."

"Sorry sir, the last bus left a half hour ago, you will have to wait till the morning."

Jacob stormed back to the car, pushed me and asked me for 10 thousand pesos. We were down to our last 80,000. "No, man, relax take a goddamn break and chill out." He shoved me and asked for the money again. I shoved him back and after a short struggle Caleb and Red pulled us away from each other. The four of us sat down covered in dirt.

After five minutes of silence, I started laughing like a maniac. It was the nerves, the booze and the canned ham. "All this shit over toilet paper." He looked at me as if I was crazy and then started laughing too. Pretty soon we all just sat there laughing, even Lucia. I went over to one of the street vendors, bought some mango juice, and we all shared as we talked about the rest of the trip. The stay at Cabo would be cheap because Luis's brother, Eduardo, ran a little chain of shacks along the shore.

About an hour away from Cabo, the road was not paved; it was all dirt and desert sand. In the middle of the night this didn't seem so bad. At least that's what we kept telling ourselves. Actually, if the car would have broken down there we would have been car-less, and helpless in the middle of the desert. The last bit of the way, the road was bumpier, and the booze had worked its magic. We ran over a hare, and decided that we would not waste precious meat, so we pulled over, with flashlights a hunting knife and no idea of what we were doing, we skinned the hare.

When we reached Cabo de la Vela, everyone had already gone to sleep except for a small group of tourists from Cartagena. They were sitting around a dying fire on the beach, and drinking the last of their rum. When they saw us pull up they brought some chairs and we joined our two groups to drink. They lit up cigarettes and joints to pass around. Lucia and Damian left to sleep first. The rest of us stayed up, drinking and smoking. In the moonlight you could see our drunken smiles, and the crabs on the shore. I decided to take a dip.

"You crazy drunk bastard don't do it," chuckled Jacob. But I had to; I shook my shoes off, and jumped in with just my boxers. I floated for a long time. I wasn't scared, and there was nothing on my mind. The water flowed through me. The sand and small waves created a soft rhythmic song. And the sky. Oh, that beautiful sky with an almost full moon. I wouldn't trade, for anything in the world, that dip in the water, that view of the sky, the soft electricity of rum that flowed through me. That night, I knew nothing, but I was content with the hum of the night, if only for that night.

Five

I sit at the riverbank, with a peaceful calm flowing through me. I know the full moon is on its way. Maybe that is what El Mamo's ceremony will do. Maybe the ceremony will bring that peace, that harmony to my whole family. I feel for my wallet and remember the little paper. I pat the wallet and say a prayer to the spirits. I ask my grandfather to help me make it to the full moon, to help me through the ceremony, and then night falls. I begin to walk upstream, with my stomach growling and churning.

I walk and begin to cough, louder and louder. I am shaking violently. Suddenly, I feel something moving in my throat. I uncover my mouth and with one last cough, my throat cleared. When I look over, I see the bright red spider. The spider struggles out of the slime, and then hurriedly climbs the tree and is lost.

I look up in disbelief. My grandfather told me of the red spider. "It climbs inside the sleeping person and makes its way into the stomach. Where all hunger comes from. There it makes a web, traps hunger and eats it. You don't get rid of hunger though until you are rid of the spider, but once it's gone you won't feel hungry ever again. Don't be fooled by this, though. You can still die of starvation, but you won't feel it."

Once I reach the sign that faintly reads "Tyronaca" on a rotting piece of wood, I place my manta by the rocks and lay in the most perfect nook. The water continues to run, and a soft mist rises from the ground as the sun comes up. All the birds are waking from their slumber, and all the bugs start their crawling. I put out the rest of my cigar and adjust my head on my manta. In the song of the morning I safely get some rest.

Six

I had been floating for so long that they thought I had drowned. So, when Jacob and Red jumped in the water to rescue me, all the peace and harmony had gone. They yanked my leg up and I felt my head drop into the water.

I tried to find the ground with my hands and managed to bring my head up for a breath, but as they dragged me, my head dropped back in. I could not breathe. I felt the air leave my lungs and I set into panic. I needed to breathe in. I kicked and flailed, until they let me go. My face broke through the water and I gasped to let the air fill my lungs. I sat for a moment in the water breathing in deeply, as though I had never breathed before.

Their drunken rescue was almost the end of me. After regaining my breath and calm I sat by the shore and puked up the ham, crackers, tequila and rum that were startled out of me, until there was nothing to throw up, and then my body just convulsed violently throwing up nothing.

With the help of Red, I got into some dry clothes and went to bed. I was breathing but the world was spinning, so I anchored my foot and hand onto the sand. It was no use. I just lay there as the room we were assigned kept spinning, and finally I fell asleep.

The next morning I woke up, and looked over at the small bedside table. On it, there was a glass of water and a small packet of Bonfiest, which dissolves any hangover or at least it claims to. I looked up and grabbed my throbbing head. At that moment, the smell of coconut oil seeped through the doorway. A thin longhaired Wayuu woman stood at the foot of my bed, with the typical gown of the Wayuu's draped over her. Her face was adorned with dark red paint and her black eyes were as deep as wells, and seemed to hold me in their depth. She walked back out, and I nodded off to sleep again.

I thought I had dreamt her, but when I awoke, I saw the packet of Bonfiest, broke it in the water and drank it eagerly. As I drank and I tried to get myself up, a giggling sunburned woman walked into the room. She had a lingering odor of stale rum. When she saw me on my bed, she laughed and made her way next to me. She kissed me, sloppily, and then walked out.

I sprung up after a moment, began to follow her. Jacob and Red must have sent her to mess with me and torture me through this hangover. I ran through the archway but the brightness of the morning hit me like a brick wall. I covered my eyes and began to work them open, all the while following the trail of laughter. I ran through the burning sand. Every step, hot as coals, shot up to my navel.

"Q'hubo Teomio, jogging off that hangover?" Jacob shouted from his seat around the table. By the looks of it, he was still drinking from the night before. Red sat by him laughing at my pained demeanor.

The white woman's laughter led me around the little shacks and by a lonely part of the beach. I stopped for a moment and stood in a shadow. I saw her from a distance, by the water no longer laughing, just sitting and looking out into the water with her toes in the moist sand and playing in the little waves.

Finally, I walked off the shadow and back onto the burning sand. I sat next to her and was relieved to be on cool sand. My feet stretched out beyond hers, and were numb for a moment in the gentle waves. We said nothing, and looked out at the restless water.

Seven

At around four in the afternoon my eyes open, I look at the light through the treetops and take a guess at the time, a few more hours and the sun will set. This gives me sometime to walk before darkness forces me to rest. The remainder of this journey cannot be done at night, the trees don't allow for the bit of moonlight to lead the way, and I cannot risk twisting an ankle. I carry nothing, only the small paper. I keep checking to see if in my pockets there is a forgotten coin, and I remember my grandfather warning me to always have money on me, "Sí, mijo, I was at the University taking classes, my mother had given me just enough to get to the campus and back by buseta. But, I got really hungry and spent my bus fare on an empanada. I began to walk home after class, but it was dark. Of course as is expected when you are walking through a dangerous part of Medellin at night, a mugger comes out and shakes me down. I respond angrily, 'Can't you see I'm broke, asshole. Why else would I be walking home?' 'Fuck you,' he retorted as he threw just enough bus fare at me."

I keep going through my pockets hoping that I can find another coin. After checking and rechecking, each thrust of my hand into the empty pockets feels more and more weakening. I reach into my back pocket and feel the wallet. The wallet holds the folded paper. The folded paper holds my mission.

I walk with my manta on my shoulder, alongside the widening creek. I know I am going in the right direction. The trail is, for the most part, easy to tread, but, the rocks are getting bigger, and there are more and more of them. Up ahead, I can see a formation of rocks. Here I decide to get some rest.

I find the most comfortable spot, which isn't very comfortable, and set down my manta. I remember that I haven't eaten properly in a while. I sit in my nest, and realize that I have tons of quartz crystals, amethyst and citrine. Like the ones my mother dangled all over the house, and on her children's necks.

When I close my eyes I dream of her. I remember the time she sat at the kitchen table at one in the morning, crying and fixing my science project, a recreation of the Martian surface. I came in quietly and grabbed her hand. She could no longer keep her tears from me. I realized through her look that she had decided not to take my father back, and I knew it pained her to see his face in mine.

I wanted her to hold me close and run, run far away. I knew her weary arms would not allow it. Her scarred knees from kneeling to clean bathrooms and stranger's houses could barely hold her up.

"Teomio," she whispered, as she moved her hand to the citrine necklace she made me, "let's finish making Mars." She handed me a small alien that she had ingeniously made with my play dough and a lightbulb. Together we finished the project. The surface of Mars had water from the rain of that late Sunday night.

Eight

I finally asked her, "Do I know you?" She smiled without turning to me, and stood up. Her bathing suit came off her and dropped onto the sand. She ran into the water, her blonde hair trailing behind. Her sun-red skin glistened with the water; I stripped down and splashed awkwardly after her.

After our ungraceful adventures in the water, she spoke in heavily accented Spanish about going to meet up with her friends again, and left. I was glad to be alone. I sat in the sand for some time. When the sand bugs started stinging me, I made my way back.

Nine

In the protection of the minerals, I sleep, for the first time in a while, during the night. The terrain is getting more difficult and I cannot risk a fall.

In the misty morning, I gather some small crystals. One of each: quartz, citrine and amethyst, and continue up the widening creek. Around noon, I feel my feet dragging. I don't feel hungry, but I know I need food. My body might shut down at any moment, but I need to keep going. I can't stop walking. My eyesight has gotten blurry, but I continue, focusing on the sound of gravel and leaves beneath me. I can't be too far from the blue rock.

Over the sound of the creek and my dragging feet, I can hear a rhythmic splash. As I get closer, I begin to hear two women talking. I know they are talking, but I cannot make out what they are saying. The closer I get the clearer their figures. They are ceremoniously washing clothes and then I realize that the creek has led me to the river. From behind me, I hear a rustling of leaves and children giggling, I see the women stand up with broad shoulders in a defensive stance but before I could speak, my knees give out, and there's nothing but darkness.

I wake up in a small room; on the wall in front of me is the painting of El Sagrado Corazón de Jesús, and a rose-colored rosary. I try to rise, and a tall man comes into the room from outside. He brings me water in a tin cup that I accept with my shaking hands and parched mouth. He hands me a bowl of calentado, a mushy mixture of beans rice and, if you're lucky, meat. This calentado has no meat. But it is the most delicious and savory meal I have ever had. My mouth salivates. I cannot eat fast enough with my weak body.

After gorging half of the mushy mixture, I look over at the man who stands at the table, in what appears to be the kitchen, ripping apart some leaves and crushing them with his fingertips. I look over and see a big clay kettle, with a steady stream of steam over a hotplate, and finally, remembering my manners I say, "Muchas gracias, señor." He doesn't look up from his leaf crushing, and instead gives me a smile from the corner of his mouth.

In a hoarse voice he replies, "You gave us quite a scare." He pours steaming water from the kettle into the bowl with the crushed leaves, and hands it to me, "Drink this, you need to regain your strength, hawthorn, ginkgo and nettle will fix you up."

When I gather enough energy to stand and walk around I realize there is only one room, the kitchen-bedroom-living room-home. The bathroom is a shared tin outhouse. The other houses look similar, rusted tin on the outside, and one small room inside. I remember hearing stories about these houses, set up many years ago by the government as promises of bigger and better homes in exchange for land. These temporary shacks became permanent homes, and the lost lands just a distant memory.

I see the man who has taken care of me. He walks over to me, "I'm glad to see you are up and about." He pats my back and motions me to walk back to the shack. "Listen, a few of us are concerned. Why don't you tell us exactly what you were up to?" I reach into my back pocket where I expect to pull out the wallet and then the folded paper. Nothing. My eyes widen and at seeing my expression the thin man points me into his home. "I think you are looking for this." There it is. Next to my wallet, the once folded sacred piece of paper that could not be touched until the full moon by the blue rock, lies on the dirty kitchen table open, violated and full of stains. The heat and anger rises into my ears. I snatch the paper, and attempt to fold it again. There's no use. It is ruined.

Ten

Back around the guadua houses, I joined Jacob with Damian on his lap, Lucia, and Red at the table. Jacob was in a drunken bragging state, waving his hunting knife around. I could see that everyone was on edge. But sleep was taking over Jacob. Before falling asleep on the weak plastic chair, he decided to move into a bed.

I walked onto the sand in front of the choza, rolled up my manta, and lay there taking in the sun. Damian splashed in the shore with his mom sitting by. Red and Caleb raced in the water and dared each other to go further out. Luis and Jacob slept, and Sirius played with Buche, the laughing dog.

Later that day, Jacob woke up; the dreadful hangover had taken a hold of him. He sat next to me, and for five minutes swore up and down never to drink again. It was late in the afternoon, and we talked about other adventures that we had been on, and planned our next adventure.

After some hours, two beautiful Guajira women came to us with their colorful mochilas and bracelets. We admired their work and their crimson red face paint, and when I attempted to say, "Nnojolaa, wayoo." I must have messed that up because they turned to each other and rolled their eyes. Then they walked away, talking and shaking their heads.

Jacob laughed and patted me on the back, "Nice try."

At that moment a car pulled up to the side of the choza, and a tall stoic Guajiro man stepped out. Two of the boys that were napping under the shade sprang up and ran to him. He ordered them around in Wayuunaiki. The boys were soon busily sweeping, hanging chinchorros and bringing water.

Once he saw that work was being done, he came over. Jacob and I got up, "I was wondering where you were," Jacob exclaimed. "This is my friend, Teomio. Teomio, this is Eduardo." We shook hands and he spoke in the most elegant Spanish. "Bienvenido, siéntase en su casa." Eduardo pulled up a chair and Jacob lay on a chinchorro across from him.

I waddled out into the water, where Lucia and Damian still played.

"We should go see the sunset from the lighthouse."

In an hour, we were packed, back in the car and making our way to the lighthouse. Eduardo stayed behind minding his hotel.

The lighthouse was a small unimpressive metal contraption; it sat atop a rocky hill, at the bottom of which they sold beer and other refreshments. We were surrounded by tourists.

On our way back, the sky was still light. On the trail, there was a car stuck in the sand. People stood by, thinking of a way to get it out. Jacob pulled the car around and set it on a spot where it would not have the same fate. Red, Jacob and I walked over. There were enough of us to push it out, but in the first attempt the tourist dug the tire deeper into the sand. "Teomio, take the wheel." The woman stepped out and blamed her husband for getting them stuck. With three big pushes, and my maneuvering, the car was free. The grateful couple shook our hands, and the rest of us clapped.

When we made it back to the hotel, it was dark. Dinner was being served, it was shrimp. When Eduardo saw that I wasn't eating, he asked if there was something I didn't like about the food. I explained that I was allergic. He gave me a sideways look and smiled, served me a plate of the shrimp, and ordered *one of the women in the kitchen. Moments later, she came out with a tomato. Eduardo cut it into two and placed it on my plate, "Okay, now you can eat. Every few bites just take a bite of the tomato."*

Jacob shook his head. On the table, he placed a medicine bottle.

"Well if that doesn't work, let's hope this does."

I ate as instructed.

After dinner, Jacob, Eduardo and I gathered in the choza. We lay on the chinchorros. He ordered one of the boys to bring a crate of beer. My tongue was swollen but we determined that I would survive, and he began to talk.

In the moment when he began to speak, his voice got deeper and seemed to come from far off. He spoke, "I am part of the Aapushana clan, and the first thing to know about the Wayuu is that we are a matriarchy. That means that my mother is Aapushana and her mother is Aapushana and so on. But over time, with the way documents work, my clan name was lost, and instead I am given my father's name. I don't know my exact age. I am somewhere between thirty and thirty five years old. I was born in my mother's house, two rancherias from here. My grandmother helped deliver me."

The crate of beers had run out. Eduardo ordered some more. "These are nice and cold," said Jacob after getting a brain freeze.

Eduardo laughed, "I keep them in a fridge that runs on a separate generator."

"And the women?" I said after a long interjection about the importance of beer.

"The women of our community own property, are politicians and hold some of the most important positions in the community. The men are usually fishermen, herders and laborers. Growing up I was taught by my father all the skills I need to know about building chozas, fishing and herding. The women make the chinchorros, mochilas, and basically anything with weaving. The young girls, when they start menstruating, are isolated and their hair is cut off. They are given some of our people's medicines to prepare them for child bearing, and to keep their breasts firm even after breast-feeding five and six kids. During this period they learn the women's trades, including cooking and being good wives. Today the seclusion period isn't as long as it once was, but after the ritual the girl is a woman. She can be married."

"Does she get to choose who she marries?" Interrupted Red, who had entered the choza undetected.

"It is up to the family. As I said before, many things have changed. For example, the families take into account the woman's feelings, many of them are urged to finish school first. And if she falls in love, the two families try to come to an arrangement. Problems arise when a woman wants to marry an alijuna, but that's a different matter.

"In any case, the man's family presents the woman's family with a seal of agreement in the form of cattle. Recently, I have seen exchange of money, but traditionally it is cattle. This is meant to be a sort of insurance. Now let's say the wife cannot bear children, or turns out to be a bad deal, the woman's family is responsible for paying a fee. In a similar way if a man is abusive and beats his wife, his family pays a fee. Now he can have as many wives as he wants, or more realistically as many wives as he can afford, because with every wife there's usually six or seven children.

"Now, if the man dies and leaves behind a wife and kids, one of his brothers has the responsibility of taking his place as husband and father. If the woman dies, a younger sister needs to fill her role as mother and wife.

"When one of us dies, there is a giant ceremony. It generally has three parts. First, the initial burial, the deceased's family has to provide food and booze to host nearly two hundred people for seven days. After the seven days, the immediate family stays with the deceased for a month."

The generator and all the lights went off. In the darkness, we worked our way through the second crate of beer. Eduardo continued as though uninterrupted, "Recently I have been expanding my search of religion. Yes, I have been reading a lot about some African religions. Yoruba religion makes sense to me. Either way I refuse to follow the evangelists, even if they pin their cross on our land."

"And the afterlife?" asked Red.

"That one is simple. There is no heaven or hell, all of that's right here." He took a long swig of his beer and rose, "Y colorín colorado este cuento se ha acabado. Hasta mañana, muchachos," and he stumbled into the night.

The next morning, the sun had just come up, and I was lying on the hammock awake, breathing in the cool morning air. Luis and Caleb brought over some breakfast. Luis put a tray in front of me and said, "Better get some food, Jacob wants us to leave today, and knowing him we'd better get ready to go." Jacob had not slept, but instead sat in the darkness of the choza drinking until it was light again. When the sun rose, he looked around, and walked into the room where Damian and Lucia were.

The rest of us grabbed our trays, but before anyone could take a bite, a deep shout came from the room, "Red, get in here." Red dropped his spoon and rushed in. After a moment, he came out shrugging at us from afar. He walked toward the car and tried to get it started. The car growled and growled, but the engine would not turn over. Red kept at it. We took our food, and walked over to him.

"Jacob wants me to get the car started. We're leaving." Luis placed the trays in the car, and raced to grab his bag from his room. Caleb stood with Red, peering into the open hood of the car. The priest came with his bag, and handed them to Caleb. Caleb climbed to the top of the car and began to tie down all the bags. Everything seemed to be ready except for the car itself. Jacob came over with Sirius. Lucia and Damian followed.

Jacob signaled them into the back seats. He handed me Sirius' leash, sat down in the front seat, brought his cap over his eyes, and began to snore.

Caleb finished tying down the bags, and climbed into the driver's seat. I put Sirius into the middle seat, and the rest of us filed behind the car to push. After only a few feet the car groaned, growled and awoke. Caleb pumped the gas and we made ourselves comfortable in the car. The priest sat directly behind Jacob by the door, but when he tried to slam it shut, *the door whipped back. Slam, slam, slam, nothing… The door refused to close. I took my manta and through Jacob's open window and the broken door's open window I tied the door closed. Caleb took off.*

After only a few minutes on the road, Jacob shifted in his seat, and snap, the seat fell back onto Luis's knee. Jacob awoke and looked around, we tried to bring the chair back up but it, like the door, was not latching. I felt around under the seat, and pulled out half of a screw. "Really? That's what was holding me up?" Jacob laughed and lay back. The seat pressed on Luis's knees and Luis began to squirm and fuss.

"This is hurting my knees. This isn't fair, man, get up. Let's switch seats or something." Jacob laughed and looked back at Luis's distress. Before Jacob could say anything, I pushed the chair up with my own knee and held it there. The shifting weight of Jacob was crushing my knee but I'd rather have my knee crushed, than hear what was behind that look of his.

My efforts were futile, because after only a few moments Jacob began to say to Luis in his mocking tone, "You sure are an unlucky bastard. Everyone in this car, except Caleb is an atheist." Luis's eyes peered at the back of Jacob's head and he began to turn red.

"I don't believe that for a second."

Jacob let out a big taunting laugh and asked in a big amplified voice, "If you believe in the Almighty God, and all the Jesus mumbo jumbo, speak up." We were silent. All our heads dropped in shame. Sirius let out a bark. "Well, look at that, there is one believer amongst us." Jacob's laugh sliced the silence of the car, and before anyone could speak, Jacob jeered, "The damned dog, we're going to have to baptize him, don't you think."

We chuckled uncomfortably. The priest was enraged, and in a low tone he said, "Let me out of the car." I looked over at him, but he couldn't see me.

Jacob's eyes shifted, "You heard him, stop the car."

Caleb protested, "Aw, man, come on, let's just get home."

"I said, stop the car."

"We can't just leave him here. This is the desert, man."

"Now."

A shrieking silence. The car came to a halt. Jacob yanked the manta from the broken door, stepped out into the sun, reached up for Luis's bag and tossed it onto the desert floor. Luis stepped out, and all he managed to say was, "Even though you treat me like this, I will pray for you all." He picked up his bag, wiped the dirt off, and began to walk back toward the sea.

"I'm not driving off without him. We can't just leave him, man." Caleb half pleaded half demanded.

Jacob shrugged his shoulders and whispered, "Then stay."

Before Jacob could make his way around to the driver's seat, Caleb extended his hand, signaled Jacob to stop and shrugged, "Ok, let's go."

Jacob walked toward the broken door signaled me into the front seat, and stretched out across the middle seats after handing me his belt pack, "The money's there. You're in charge now. Get us home." His trunk like leg held up the broken seat. I tied the door closed with my manta lay my back against the door, and Caleb pulled off.

The priest disappeared in the trail of dust we left behind.

Eleven

I look over at my host, my eyes piercing through him. He takes a step back, and raises his hands between us. He begins to plead, but I cannot hear him past the blood that is pounding in my ears. I look down, the writing on the note is like that of a 7 year-old, and in pencil scribbled and rushed on two lines is written, "Qué le dijo una chancla a la otra? 'Ombe que vida tan arrastrada." I could see El Mamo in his dark library, dropping books into piles and laughing.

"We just wanted to know who you were," my host pleaded.

"Do you know where the blue rock is?" I asked after closing my eyes for a moment.

"What do you mean? Like a mine?" The paper crushed in between my fingers.

"No. Just one big blue rock, it's supposed to be by the river."

"Well, hermano there's nothing like that around here. Maybe it's further upstream. May I ask why you are looking for a blue rock?"

"I don't know. I just know I have to find it. That damn Mamo probably made up the rock story."

"Mamo? What are you talking to a mamo for?" I walk over to the bed and sit. My host follows and sits on the stool from where he had fed me to health.

"Listen, I'm not supposed to be telling you this. If the other people here found out what you're up to they would beat some sense into you. We are Christian people, and that Santeria has no room here. But, there's this really strange blind man that lives about thirty minutes up stream. I can draw you a map. They exiled him because he tried bringing that stuff here. The only reason they didn't kill him was because they were scared that he might curse us."

He walks over to the small kitchen, grabs a pencil crushed by teeth marks and holds out his hand to me. I hand him the crushed paper, which he flattens out. First he draws the river, then his little village, two simple arrows, one upstream following the river the other into the woods, which he signals by drawing trees. At the point where the second arrow turns into the woods he draws a tree with a dagger on it. Next to the old man's house he writes his name, and says out loud, "Se llama Gilberto."

He folds the paper over twice, and hands it to me. I hold it between my fingers for a while before putting it into my shirt pocket.

"I guess I must be off, then." He holds his index finger up to me, and hurries into the kitchen. He opens a tub on the counter that serves as a cupboard, and brings out a package with dried fruits inside. He closes the lid and lifts the little stove. From under it, he pulls out a similar leaf-wrapped package, opens it, then pauses for a moment. He looks over at me, smiles weakly, closes the package and puts it next to the fruits. By the sink, there is an old rag, which he lays on the counter. He places the packages on the center and ties the four corners forming a small bag. He then goes out by the side of the house and comes back in with an ancient water bottle tied to a string. It was filled with a brownish liquid. He hands me the package and water and walks with me by the river.

"Good luck, hermano, see you in better times." I tie the little bag to my belt, nod my head and walk off, not once looking back.

Twelve

We had driven about 20 minutes on the dirt road when the windmills appeared in the distance. After passing the windmills we would get back onto paved highway and it would be my turn to drive. Everyone in the car was wide-awake except for Jacob whose snores filled the otherwise quiet car. I tried to fiddle with the radio but all we got was static, I shut it off. Caleb looked over at me, "I really hope this car makes it. It's already starting to fall apart."

When we finally pulled out of the desert dirt road Caleb pulled over and we switched seats. I knew I had to drive all the way back but without the stop in Maicao, Valledupar and the Finca the trip would be reduced to just about six hours.

Stalling at least half a dozen times before getting the hang of driving stick shift again, I began to get going. I drove and kept a steady and speedy pace. A few moments on the paved road and everyone, except Caleb, slept.

Once we had followed the road to the main highway the intersection was busy with people, food, gasoline and American clothing shops. I pulled over and had a young kid just about 12 years old fill up the car with one of the cheap gasoline containers. I grabbed 40 thousand pesos, paid the boy and we were on our way again.

The sun started to set; we were about half way back when I had to stop for a leak. Caleb and I were the only ones awake, so I pulled to the side of the road, ran to take care of business and ran back in to the car ready to get home.

Hitting that first gear is always tricky, and once again the engine stalled on me. The second time however, when I did get the gears right, the car shot forward and jolted back. I tried turning the car off and starting it again. Nothing.

I looked in the rearview, everyone was awake from the jolt. "Try starting it on second gear" Jacob's voice came from the silent darkness. The car crawled forward and picked up momentum, but it wouldn't go past 40 mph. We were happy to just get it moving. We all sat quietly listening to the engines weak and almost lifeless moaning.

The road began to turn and twist, and the hills got bigger and bigger. The car would slow to a weak 10 mph on every rise. At this pace, we began to make our way up the mountain. The trees made the night darker. The thickening foliage obscured the moon. We crawled in the night with the ticking of the emergency lights, and the groans of our dying car.

We were still about two and a half hours away from home. I knew we weren't going to make it. Every hill seemed to be our last. It wasn't until we had finished descending and climbing half way up the next hill that the car shut off and began to roll backwards. I yanked the emergency brake and the car halted, and then inched back slowly. Jacob untied the door, stepped out, and stretched, "Ok, we can't leave it here, a car or truck 's bound to come by and in these hills they won't have time to see us. Everyone out." Jacob walked over to the driver's side, and in a tired and concerned tone said, "Alright, you get out and push. I'll guide the car onto the side of the road. From there we can figure out what our next step is." I stepped out and got behind the car with Red and Caleb. Lucia stood on the side with Damian and Sirius. We pushed. The muscles in my back clenched tight but the car didn't budge.

"Get the emergency brake, man!" I shouted at Jacob.

He laughed, "Oh, my bad." Still, the car barely moved. I looked over at Caleb as Jacob set the brake again. "Let's just let it slide back." I walked to Jacob, "Alright, so when I say so, you release the break and we're going to get it in reverse."

Jacob nodded, and I set my hands just under the back window. I knocked on the window and heard the creak of the released break, and we let the car slide back. Jacob maneuvered the car as far off the road as possible without going into the roadside ditch.

This was still a bad spot to be in. Any car speeding down could clip the car and send us flying. We decide to climb over the ditch, onto a mound of grass not too close to the trees. Jacob came by me and reached in the belt pack. He pulled out a box of matches and popped the hood of the car. Just then, a bright pair of headlights drew near, slowing. Like frightened deer we stared without moving. The headlights passed us and the 18-wheeler pulled up in front of our broken down car. Jacob and Red disappeared by the driver's side of the truck while the rest of us waited on the mound by the trees.

After just a few moments three men returned: Jacob, Red and the truck driver. "Alright, Teomio. Look around for some rope. We have to tie her up. This gentleman is going to give us a lift to his house where he's got more tools to help us out." I head to *the back of the car and look around under the back seats, nothing but empty bottles. I dig around every nook and cranny of the car, in the glove compartment, under the front seats. Nothing. I return to the group empty handed. "There's nothing."*

After a while of thinking and looking around Caleb asks, "You think we can tie her up with our belts?" I laugh at the thought, but the group proceeded to hand in their belts. I hooked my tattered brown leather belt, to the front bumper of our tragedy machine, to the back of the 18-wheeler. Jacob hands me his black and gray nylon belt, I manage to rope it around twice. Red and Lucia's belts followed. The car was as secure as it could be. Caleb, Red and I stayed in the car, while the rest made their way into the cabin of the truck. Soon, the truck began to move and the three of us followed. Caleb smiled, "I hope this guy's not planning on mugging us."

"What's he going to do, steal our car?"

Caleb let out a laugh, still his eyes narrowed and his expression was as serious as ever. Red lay down and covered his eyes with his forearm. I kept the van steady behind the moving truck. It flowed up and down the hills, my foot on the break to keep the two vehicles from bumping together.

Thirteen

I continue to follow the river. Dizzy from looking at the trees. Did I pass the dagger and miss it? I keep walking, not from my own choice but because my feet keep going. They seem to lead me. They are not light and feathery; instead they are heavy, like cinderblocks.

Then, I see it. At first I think that I have imagined it, and it takes a minute before my eyes adjust. It is an old blade, the handle made of wood, painted in blue. The paint is chipped, and the wood cracked, the blade rusted and brown. Before I turn and head into the forest, I walk to the river bank.

My legs are shaking, so I sit and put the water bottle down. I take off my zapatos and socks. I dip my feet into the running water. The water that flows from the sierra is cold as ice. And soon my feet are numb. The soles of my feet, hard and coarse, desperately absorb the water. I fold my pants up just below my knees, and move my feet around and around over the rocks. I dig my hands into the rocks under the cold river water. The cool rocks, surrounds my rough hands. I dig and dig through the rocks until I hit the mud. I grasp a handful of the powdery soil, and rub my hands together.

Fourteen

We pulled up to a house. The van climbed onto the gravel driveway, and the three of us that followed in the van stepped out. The truck driver quickly came around back and let the others out of the compartment. Jacob handed Sirius over to me, and all of us waited as the man ran into the house and back out with a rusty toolbox. Caleb, Jacob and the truck driver got to work. What they planned to do, I had no clue.

Suddenly Sirius began to jump. He barked and ran around. He bit at the ground, and tugged and tugged, until we were away from the group, on the other side of the car. He barked and bit at his paws. "What's wrong boy?" Pretty soon I found out. Lucia was the first to scream. She ran and slapped at her legs. "Hijueputa!" Then like a domino effect everyone felt them. The fire ants.

Sirius was barking and snapping at the few that were still on him, but he had pulled me safely away from their trail. The rest of the group saw me laughing and ran by where Sirius had dragged me. I tried to get nearer to the ants to see them, but Sirius was not having it. He barked at me and would not budge. I was close enough, however, to see the trail of ants, busily going about their business.

The truck driver, Caleb and Jacob were still at the car, working on it, glancing over, mocking the hysterical Lucia. The truck driver and apparently amateur mechanic was pulling apart the car, and putting together a pretty questionable contraption. He tied a tube from under the car and emerged it into a pimpina of gasoline that he brought out from his house.

"Alright. Now you just have to drive it slowly. This should get you to Santa Marta, but just to be safe I can take some of you in the truck. It's only about two-and-a-half-hour drive."

Jacob looked at Lucia, "I'll go with them. Teomio, you can drive the van. If anything comes up, there are a few towns on the way. Someone should lend you their phone."

Caleb and Red nodded at each other. Caleb suggested, "Red and I should stay with Teomio. The rest of you get home, and we will call you if anything comes up."

I stood by the van helping them unload, and Jacob came to me, "Thanks for doing this, man. It's best if I get them back home. Here's the last of the trip money, it's not much."

Fifteen

I soak my hands and feet in the water, and bring the icy water up to my face. After I wash my face I take a drink of the cool river. It runs down my chin, and onto my chest and then I hear it.

A Mariamulata of black feathers and yellow eyes stares at me from the other side of the river. She puffs up, and lets out a tiny screech, and stares at me. She jumps in a little dance closer and closer until she is by the water. She takes a drink. I can see on her wing a cluster of aqua-blue feathers. But before I could make out the shape or figure, she flies up and past me. She swoops back around me, eyeing me from all directions, and then balances atop the dagger on the tree.

And then I remembered the story of the Mariamulata. I could hear my mom screaming,

"Get away from that nest. She's going to peck your eyes out." It was well known among my friends and all the adults that one must never disturb a Mariamulata's nest. She would find you and peck your eyes out. But the story goes far back. My grandfather sat in his rocking chair peeling an orange and the story came, "This story goes back to when the Spaniards were trading and selling slaves. The slaves came shackled, starving and beaten. Once they were, they tried their best to make homes out of prisons.

"One young mulata, María, took to caring and looking after the birds. One night, when she was around nine, the Spaniard crept into the barn where she and the other children slept. He raised the oil lamp and looked around and made his way to the trembling María. After tearing off her clothes and forcing himself on her, María let out a loud screech.

"At first they sounded like a light summer breeze. But soon they sped around like a storm and began to swarm like wasps. In minutes they had him surrounded. In a choreographed dance they pecked his eyes out. They didn't stop until they were through with him."

The Mariamulata puffs up and lets out another much louder screech that deafens me, and then slowly and in big dips she flies in the direction I need to go. I pat my feet dry with the manta, slip on my socks and zapatos, grab the water bottle and continue walking.

Sixteen

I put the old Volkswagen into 4th gear. It crawled down the hill picking up pace and momentum much needed to make the next hill. Red was in the back seat holding the pimpina above his head. The plastic tube from the container guzzled the gasoline directly to something under the car.

This was the contraption that the truck driver made to get us moving. He drove in front of us, and we followed, ready to be left behind at any moment.

We sat in silence for fear that the car would hear our voices, and everything would go wrong.

The four others rode in the container of the truck in front of us. At least they would make it back. We crawled up the second hill. The car was down to a weak drifting, the pimpina was down to its last gulps and we were still two hours away from home.

The car had almost reached the top of the third hill when it stopped. We watched the truck disappear into the night. Red put down the pimpina. I tried to start the car again. Red opened the door and stepped out, "It's no use, let's get her off the road before we get rear ended."

Caleb followed him to the back of the car. I released the emergency break. We got the little van to the peak of the hill. Caleb and Red hopped in to the moving van, it caught speed downhill and Caleb pointed, "There." He pointed to an enormous house with a huge lawn. On the lawn of the house by the road there was a little shed. We parked beside it. I stepped out, stretched, and lit a cigarette. Red went around looking for big rocks to place behind the tires, and then came over to have a smoke. We all shared the pack. The lights of the house were off. The nearest town was at walking distance, but everything was closed when we passed it earlier. We had to give Jacob enough time to get home. We would have to wait until tomorrow to try to make a call.

In the morning Jacob and the rest of them would reach Santa Marta, they would surely send us some help. Red came over to us and handed me a comforter. "Cover the other side. We should get some rest. Too much movement is sure to attract the wrong people."

I nodded, "I hope they don't mind us camping on their lawn." I walked over to the driver's side of the van, and over the missing window I draped the comforter. The mosquitos were out and violently attacking.

Red climbed under the blanket. I lay my head on the manta. The soft snoring began to fill the car, and so, I fell asleep.

Seventeen

After about twenty minutes of walking I see it, the small clay house, with hay roof. Out of the hole in the roof there's a trail of white smoke. The heavy smell of sage lingers in the air. Before I knock, the door swings open. A small lady with disheveled, gray hair, stands there, looking at me. She wears a simple beige dress, but her chest is adorned with several elaborate beaded necklaces made with aquamarine stones, citrine, quartz and just about every stone I could remember. She opens her eyes wide, places her hands high on her hips and waits. It takes me a while, before I can speak, "Umm...Uh. Is Gilberto here?"

"It's Gilber-taa. Now come along, you've been taking your sweet time to get here." She pulls me into a chair and walks over to the stove. Gilberta's house is very much like the house of the man who sent me this way. On the table there is a small green oil lamp, a wooden bowl of aging fruit and a leather bound notebook with yellowed paper.

She walks over to the stove, dips a cup into the pot and cleans it off with the rag by the stove. She then walks over to me. The sweet smell of aguapanela makes my mouth water. I sip on the warm sweet drink and remember home.

"You have something for me." She drinks from her cup and holds her other hand out to me. I pass her the water bottle, and untie the bag that the man had prepared. She puts the bottle on the table and uncaps it. She finishes her drink and in the same cup pours some of the water. She then takes the bag from me, and lays out all its contents. I stand by her, she is much shorter than me, but her spirit and authority can hardly be contained in the room.

The rag on the table holds a ball of hair, some crystals and dried leaves. Gilberta grabs the hair and tosses it in the water. She takes the leaves and crushes them into flakes in her hand and drops them into the water. Finally, she picks up one of the crystals and licks it. She mumbles, and walks over to the counter with the crystals in hand. She grabs a big flat rock and a smaller one.

She places the clear cube of crystals over the flat rock, and with the smaller one begins to crush them and work them into a fine powder, which she then brushes into the cup.

She dusts off her hands on her dress, sighs and then says, "Now tell me what are you looking for."

"The uh... blue rock."

"Nonsense. There's no blue rocks around here. What are you looking for?"

I took out the wrinkled paper with the map and the joke, from my wallet, and handed it to her, "El Mamo sent me here to look for a blue rock. I was supposed to open this there at the full moon."

She looks at the paper, mumbles the joke and lets out a loud laugh.

"You're looking for something that doesn't exist." She finally says. "But what do you do when you need something that doesn't exist?"

I look down at her cup of strange mixture, and look back at her quizzically.

She slams her fist down on the table, "You make it! If you want or need the world to be blue, you paint it blue. That is all."

She grabs the cup and mixes the ball of hair around in the flakes and the dissolving powder. Then she rips of a piece of the rag, wraps the ball of hair up, and hands it to me.

"Here, when you go paint your rock blue, I need you to bury this at the foot of it." She walks over to the door and steps out. I follow her. "Just keep following the path that brought you here. The main road is a twenty-minute walk. Then make a left. Across from the hardware store, you will see another trail that in only a few minutes will get you to the river. Buy the paint, paint the rock, and your ceremony is complete. Oh, and don't forget my package. It's very important." She takes from my hand the cup that I was still holding. She hands me a 5 thousand pesos bill and stands at her doorway waving me along.

I walk. This time a lot less hopeful than I was before, and a lot more confused. I need to paint the rock blue, and then I need to bury the package. The package seems to have nothing to do with my own ceremony. Still, it has to be done. I just want it to end, beat the evil, tame the spirits and go home. I walk on, reach the main road, and turn left to find the tiny hardware store.

Eighteen

I woke up to a quiet morning, a sweaty back, and mosquito bites all over my legs. Caleb was climbing out of the car when he saw that I was awake. "I'm going into town to see if I can reach Jacob, or a tow truck."

I climbed out after him, and we lit the last cigarette. We passed it back and forth, without the discomfort of small talk. Then, as if from the morning mist, they emerged. Three scrawny and mean looking barefoot men in shorts carrying large double barrel shot guns. The cigarette trembled in my hand, so I put it to my mouth and took a long swig. Through the smoke I squinted at the approaching men.

Caleb held out his hand, "Good morning, hermano. Our car broke down here last night. Sorry to be on your land."

The man that seemed to be in charge met Caleb's hand and smiled, "Ah, there's no problem. If we can help just let me know."

The man turned and signaled to the other two. They nodded to us and followed him to the house. Within a few minutes the silent and dormant house came alive. Kids were running and chasing each other, some came to look at our broken down car turned campsite.

I gave Caleb the money that Jacob had left me, and he took off into town. Red climbed out rubbing his eyes. I reached into the van and stuck my hand in all the crevices to look for loose change. Red and I turned out our pockets and managed to get about 2 thousand pesos. When Caleb returned, he gave us the change; altogether we had about 9 thousand pesos. Jacob wasn't answering, and the tow truck would take about an hour and a half. Which means just about three hours.

No point in sitting around. We closed up the van. Caleb nodded at one of the men that sat in a wicker chair in the porch of the house. He nodded back.

The 9 thousand pesos got us one bowl of soup in an old lollipop container, one pack of cigarettes (free matches), a two-liter soda, and a roll of toilet paper. We sat on the wooden steps of the store, gathered our supplies and sat in a circle passing around the soup.

The store was busy with people going in and out for groceries. Most of them just walked past us without noticing, a few of them looked with curiosity. Among the curious was a group of travelers like us that arrived to the store in an almost broken down jeep. Drunk loud and obnoxious, like us. One of the guys, thin yet athletic, came over to us. He pointed at our soup. Before he could speak, I shrugged, "This is what road trips do to you." He laughed, smiled at us, passed around his bottle of aguardiente for us to drink. "We've only just started and we're already at each other's throats."

I handed him his bottle back and thanked him. He nodded his head with a big smile, and wished us luck in making it back, before he ran back into the store that smelled like smoke.

After we had finished our soup, and had our after lunch smoke, we headed to the river. We took a dip then lay on the banks drinking the last of the booze. The smell of marijuana surrounded us. The sound of the river lulling us, the afternoon hummed.

The traveler that we met earlier wobbled into the river, from the opposite riverbank, cursing and talking to himself. Caleb and Red grumbled and snored. So I sat perched up against a tree, barely able to hold myself up and looked out into the water at him. His pale skin began to turn colors in the freezing

*water. In his hand he held the media de aguardiente.
He chugged it and as he dipped in the river the hand
with the bottle remained above water. Then, in one of
his dips, his perfectly dry hand followed. After some
time, his face broke through the water and he took one
big gasp for air. I watched the water, and in a few
moments much further down the river I saw his
flailing arms, and the top of his head, the hair sticking
up like Alfalfa's. A roaring laughter took over me. His
skinny limbs, and flailing legs were like a Sunday
morning cartoon. I laughed and laughed
uncontrollably, until Caleb and Red awoke. They
looked around and over to me, and I just pointed. Red
saw the hands that were fading into the water and ran
into the river. The seemingly calm river had dragged
him further and further down. When I no longer saw
the traveler's hands, my laughter faded, and sunk
into a pit in my stomach.*

*Red dove in, Caleb waited at the bank. I struggled
to get up. Red let the strong current take him closer
to the traveler, and when he got near him he tried to
keep him from floating further away. The heavy body
remained under water as Red struggled to free
himself and the traveler from the current. Finally,
Red caught his body in front of a boulder and was able
to pull the traveler from the water. Caleb had been
following them along the riverbank and was able to
drag them both out of the river. Why wasn't the*

traveler moving? Caleb kneeled over him and tried to bring him back. This was not the first dead man I had seen, so I quickly realized what was happening.

Red ran to the shack were we had gotten our soup, and called for help. The ambulance came, and the traveler was placed into the dreaded black bag. When they took him away, I still had not spoken. That was my last laugh.

Did you know that a moment was a medieval unit of time? Forty moments made an hour. In a medieval moment, I let the traveler drown.

It was time to head back. Jacob had completely forgottenabout us. He must have gotten home and needed to sleep for five days, he does that after the long drinking sprees.

First, we leave the priest behind in the desert and far from home stranded. Then, three of us, stuck with a useless car on a mountain surrounded by men with weapons. And finally, that moment that haunts me, that fills my lungs with water in the middle of the night. The image of the traveler drowning doesn't disappear under a night of binge drinking and his scream is ever more clear in an afternoon of uppers and downers.

The tow truck arrived and Jacob still would not pick up his phone. We knew we couldn't guarantee to pay for the truck. We asked one of the locals to watch *the car for us. We pushed it into their fence in yard, and convinced them to let us borrow enough money for three bus fares to get us back. The car of course was the security. I followed Caleb and Red around, unable to speak. We hitched about 30 minutes before a bus stopped for us. The hazy and lazy ride home took the last bit of energy from me, but I made it home. That's all that mattered then. Home.*

Nineteen

I get the can of blue paint and start walking toward the river. This is it. The last leg of my trial is almost over. All that's left is painting the rock blue. I find the small pathway in the trees, and as I am about to take my first step I hear a loud and deep laugh.

Before I turn around, I know who it is. Jacob. What the hell is he doing here? "Teomio, what the hell are you doing here? Oh, someone told me, some kind of ceremony, trying to cleanse all the shit out of your life." He comes over with his slow and confident stride. His head knocks back as he lets out another loud laugh.

I feel weakened, and I cannot help but clench my fist around the metal handle of the paint can. "I've got to get going," my voice cracked and quivered.

I could feel him reading me. It gave him power. "Well, I'm here on a mission too. From God, some might say. Ha! I have to paint some rock red, down there by the river. You look surprised." His breath reeks of rum, and stale arepa. While he speaks he jingles his car keys in his hand.

I close my eyes and start to turn away from him, "I have to get going."

He winks and inches toward the door, "I'll see you in a bit," and heads into the hardware store.

I rush to my blue rock. No paintbrushes. I dip my still shaky hands into the paint, and begin. I don't even bother to remove my clothing to save it from the paint. I splatter the paint on the rock and all around it. Then once every inch of it is covered. I take out Gilberta's little package. I plant it under the rock and then sit. It is almost done. The sun is setting, and soon it will all be over.

The sky reddens and begins to turn purple. I hear a rustling. My seat under the tree's shade hides me. So I sit still, not moving a muscle, and then I see him. Jacob. He is carrying a paint can. It is true; he is going to paint over my blue rock. He kneels by my rock, and takes the lid off his paint.

"Don't do that," I finally say just before he could splash the paint over the rock.

He chuckles and sighs, "I have to. That's too bad that this turned out like this." He raises his paint soaked hand toward the rock again.

I rise. "I can't let you do that."

"I'm going to do it, Teomio."

I grab his wrist before he can smear the red paint on my rock. He stands up, and towers over me. I do not let his wrist go, but with the hand that I held, the one covered in paint, he grabs my neck and lifts me up. My back is pressed against the tree, my feet barely on the ground. I am weak under his hold. I cannot move from his grasp. The red paint drips down my neck and onto my shirt. "Here's the problem we have. You've got your little ritual to do, and I have mine, and I'm finishing mine."

He lets me go, and I barely catch myself. By the time he walks back to the rock, kneels down and picks up the paint can, I have regained my balance and lunge at him. He loses his balance, and before he or I could react the can falls over. Splashing red paint all over my blue rock. His eyes open wide, and then with a big smile on his face he regains balance and continues to work the paint onto the rock. My rock. No, his rock is red. The sun sets. The last of my energy, gone. I sit with my back to the still wet rock. He sits next to me. Laughing, then silent. After some time he puts his hand on my shoulder, stands, and leaves without so much as a word.

I can't move. So I sit for three days.

I can see and feel the sun rise and set through the foliage. I can feel my body start to dry and wither. The paint has long dried to my shirt.

On the third day, she comes. The Mariamulata, the one with the blue patch of feathers on her wing. She stands at the river bathing, and jumping about. She bathes in the river, and only after she is clean does she turn to me. She hops closer and closer, in her little dance, tilting her head this and that way. Then she was close enough where I could see the blue X on her wing.

She hovers in the air, not very high above the ground and in a dip lands on my shoulder. She softly pecks at my ear lobe and I stand. I walk to the river, drink some water, and she remains with me. We begin our journey home.

My grandfather looked peaceful, but only for a moment. By the time anyone arrived, I had shaken him violently, and broken three ribs from the CPR. I floated through the rest of the night, as a series of people explained what came next. The days after blend in my memory. A wave of plump, sunburned faces of the relatives that he hadn't seen in years filled the wake. The smell of tanning lotion and bug spray lingered in the room. I left the service early and did not want to return to the empty house, so I sat a nearby tienda drinking until closing. When I arrived at the house, I flicked on the radio. There was a soccer match; I don't remember who was playing. It didn't matter. I let the hum of the match fill the house. I still felt alone.

Ediciones *El pozo*
Oneonta- New York

www.ingramcontent.com/pod-product-compliance
Lightning Source LLC
Chambersburg PA
CBHW020423130626
46549CB00006B/2713